LITTLE WAHIDA PUBLICATIONS

# <u>Acknowledgments</u>

My parents, Robert and Carla Brown;
My Siblings, Jordan Brown, Brittney Brown, Deshon Brown;
My Grandparents, Grandma Nedda Ann Evans, Grandma Kathy
Ann Brown-Homes, Papa Lieu Sandy Homes, Grandpa Robert
Chandler (Caesar); My Two Aunties, Aunt Edith Sutphin (Sis),
Aunt Berta Clark; My Cousins, Wahida Clark, Little Wahida Clark,
Hasana Clark; and My Teacher, Cindy Weaver

Wahida Clark Presents Publishing
PO BOX 383
Fairburn GA 30213
1(866)-910-6920
www.wclarkpublishing.com

Library of Congress Cataloging-In-Publication Data:

Chance A. Brown
Attack on Blobville: The Return of Byboom

ISBN 13-digit 978-1-957954-22-6 (paper)
ISBN: 978-1-957954-25-7 (EBOOK)

Cover design and layout by Noipoi & Nuance Art, LLC
Illustrated By Noipoi & Nuance Art
Edited by Alan Nixon
Proofreader: Carla A. Brown
Printed in the USA

# ATTACK ON BLOBVILLE:

## The Return of Bydoom

Written & Created by Chance A. Brown

Illustrated By Noipoi & Nuance Art

Once upon a time in the dimension of Pitzel, trillions of light years away from Earth, there lived a boy named Eric and his parents, King and Queen Blob.

Eric and his parents lived in a town called Blobville. King Blob is a powerful King who always has a plan to protect Blobville and Queen Blob's beautiful ruby crown.

King Blob spent several years empowering Blobville to mend from Bydoom's destruction and mayhem. Bydoom and his partner, Nooloo, a 300-foot Dinoblob, are the most dangerous villains in the Pitzel dimension.

While everyone was busy working and building new shops, restaurants, and houses, King Blob called a Blobville national meeting. Everyone was confused and wondered why King Blob was having a national meeting.

King Blob announced over the intercom, "All the people of Blobville, we will build a 400-foot wall surrounding Blobville. Is there anyone who has questions?"

Gary, a townsman, raised his hand and asked, "Why do we have to build a 400-foot wall? That will be a lot of work for a long time."

King Blob then reminded Gary and the rest of the Blobville townspeople that Nooloo is a 300-foot Dinoblob. So, the wall must be tall enough to protect against Nooloo's entry. The crowd gasped and let out a big, "OOOOHHHHHH."

"Okay, Blobsville townspeople," commanded King Blob, "let's get to work on that 400-foot wall."

The next morning, Eric, who was playing on his iBlob, shouted, "Yes! New high score!!!"

"Oh, good job! What are you playing?" inquired King Blob.

"I'm playing *Blob on the Run*," Eric replied.

"Hey, you didn't sweep the floor yesterday," King Blob observed.

"I know," answered Eric who then went to sweep the floor and do his other chores.

While Eric was doing his chores, he heard, "ROAAAAAAAAAAR!!!!"

"ROAAAAAAAAAAR!!!!"

"WOW! WHAT WAS THAT?!?" Eric asked.

"I DON'T KNOW!" Queen Blob said as she turned on the siren.

13

"ROAAAR!!!"

"Attention, all people of Blobville. I am Bydoom. Nooloo and I have come back from 1,000 years ago."

15

"You Blobs better start running because I have something new to show you. My new and improved minion-atizer."

"No! Please, No! Don't Zap Us," said a random lady.

Bydoom zapped her, "ZAP!"

"NOOOO..." the lady yelled.

17

Just then, Bydoom's Blob robot minions appeared . . .

"I am Bydoom's minion," one of them exclaimed, "and I will only take his commands."

Bydoom yelled, "Yes! My creation works! My minions are all obedient."

"Minions, All I want is Queen Blob's bright, red ruby from her crown."

"You will not take my ruby," Queen Blob said. "Okay then, I'll just take you then! Bwhahahahahaha!" said Bydoom.

"NO. DON'T TAKE ME!! screamed Queen Blob.

"Queen Blob, RUUUUUUN!" said King Blob.

Queen Blob wasn't fast enough. Bydoom grabbed the Queen and began zapping everyone who was in his path.

"Zap, zap, zap, you. Zap, you, and you!" declared Bydoom who was pleased. "Good, Nooloo. I grabbed the Queen; now let's get out of here!"

23

All over the village there were fires, broken buildings, and a massive hole in the wall.

"Is everybody okay? Eric, ERIC, WHERE ARE YOU?!!" asked King Blob.

"Over h-here, D-D-Dad . . .*cough cough*."

"OMG, ERIC, ARE YOU okay?!?!"

"Y-y-yes," answered Eric who was stuck under debris from the wall breach.

King Blob said, "Don't worry, son. I have a plan."

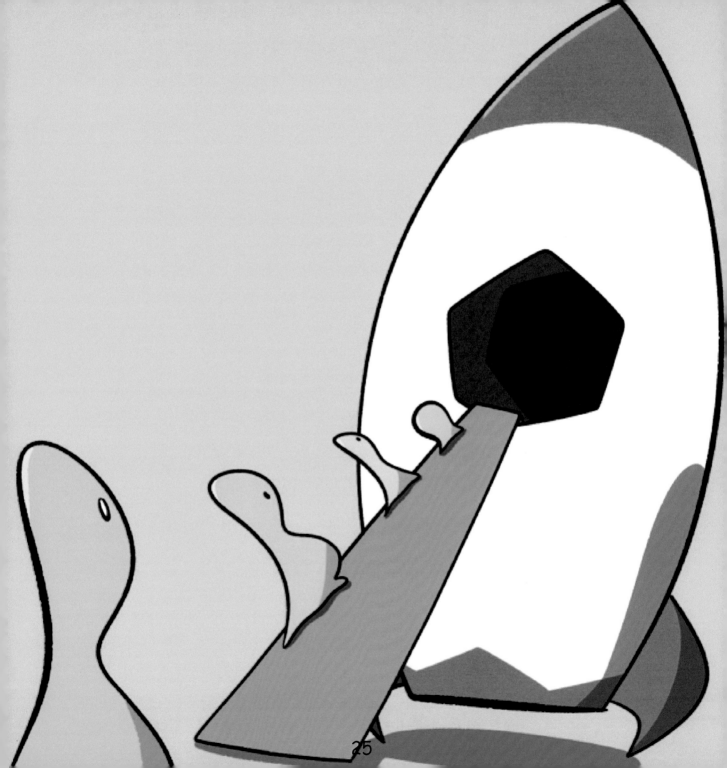

King Blob shared his plan with the Blobville blobs, and everyone prepared to save the Queen. So, everybody got on the rocket ship and went to the planet Ozze, the site of Bydoom's secret lair.

When King Blob arrived at Bydoom's secret lair, he saw that the blobs from Blobville were ready to help. He landed the ship and told everyone to get to their positions.

29

King Blob instructed, "Gary and Leo, begin distracting the guards. Strike up a conversation."

"Hey, everybody. How's your day going?" Gary asked.

"Yeah, how's your day going?" chimed in Leo.

"Me and Leo were wondering what's better, tacos or pizza...?" Gary continued.

While Leo and Gary were distracting the guards, King Blob, Eric, and Eric's friend, William, sneaked inside the lair.

When they got into the lair, they saw Nooloo standing in front of a steel door.

King Blob said, "William, do you have the bone?"

"I do," said William.

"Ok, 3...2...1...! Throw it!"

Nooloo jumped up and ran to the bone. It felt like an earthquake in the room.

When Nooloo ran for that bone, he left the steel door unprotected. King Blob's plan worked and he and the townspeople ran for the steel door.

When they got inside the steel door, King Blob saw Queen Blob, who was stuck in an ice cube, with a laser beaming the perimeter of the ruby on her crown.

"Oh, no! How do we stop the beam?" gasped Eric.

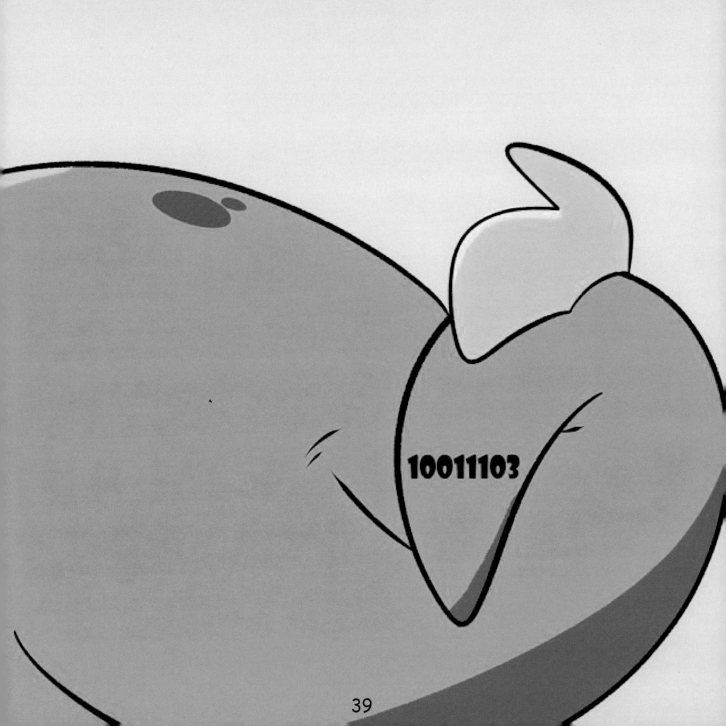

"You have to put in a code, but I don't know it," said Queen Blob.

"Wait a minute. I think I did see a code on Nooloo's tail. It said 10071103; try putting that in!" said William. "YES, IT WORKED!" he shouted.

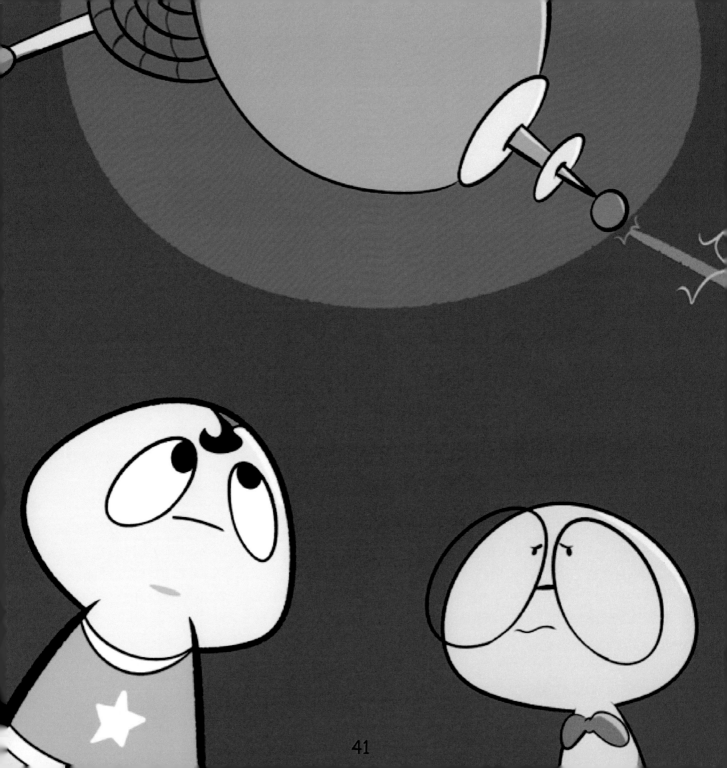

"William," King Blob said, "Oh, no! How are we going to get Queen Blob out of the ice cube?"

"Oh, not so fast! I have the heater right here," said Bydoom.

"Oh, no! It's Bydoom."

43

"Yes, I'm Bydoom, and I got the heater, and you don't! Ha ha ha!" Bydoom taunted.

45

"Eric, go turn on the laser again!" commanded William.

"Why?" Eric asked.

"Because when you do, you will cut off Bydoom's arm, and he will drop the heater," William explained.

"Won't that hurt him, though?" asked Eric.

"No, he's a blob; his arm will grow back in 7-9 hours," William said.

"Ok, here I go," Eric said as he turned on the laser.

"Grab the heater!!!" William shouted.

"Okay, burn the ice! Yay, we did it!!! Now it's time to undo the ZAP on the other Blobs and caste a ZAP Spell on Bydoom and Nooloo. A spell that will make them respect the citizens of Blobville. The ZAP Spell will make Bydoom and Nooloo rebuild the city and clean up the mess."

Both Bydoom and Nooloo were locked up in a cage made of titanium.

The citizens of Blobville lived happily ever after.

# The End

By

Chance A. Brown

LITTLE WAHIDA PUBLICATIONS

Do you have a child author in your family?
Is there a child illustrator in your home?

Would you love to have your child author/illustrator
publish a book like this one?

Little Wahida Publications Presents
Little Author and Publisher Master Class
Learn More!

Scan the QR Code or email wahida@bookcoach.com

# About the Author

Chance A. Brown, affectionately known as a military brat, was born in Daegu, South Korea where both his parents served in the US Army. By the time Chance was ten years old, he lived in three countries and five cities.

Having attended both the Department of Defense (DoD) and US public school systems, Chance gained an excellent foundation for writing.

Chance's hobbies include participating in sports and playing video games. Typically a quiet kid, he doesn't shy away from a little trash talk with his friends while dribbling on the basketball court or running up and down on the football and soccer fields.  His favorite football team is the Philadelphia Eagles, and he avidly follows his favorite basketball team, the Golden State Warriors. Whether playing on the court or manipulating the controllers, Chance is passionate about his game. As a matter of fact, he fancies himself as the ultimate slayer on *Madden*, *2K*, *Fortnight*, *Rocket League* and *Roblox* -- especially when he plays against his dad. Like Garfield, Chance's favorite meals include lasagna and cheeseburgers.

In the future, Chance aspires to write a sequel to his book, *The Attack on Blobville: The Return of Bydoom*, become a wide receiver for the University of Texas, El Paso, and, ultimately, get drafted to the NFL.

Lightning Source UK Ltd.
Milton Keynes UK
UKRC030435281222
414412UK00006B/86